PENGUIN BOOKS

ALBERT NOBBS

George Moore was born in Ireland in 1852. At the age of eighteen, following the death of his father, he ran off to Paris to study painting. Immersed in Parisian café society, he mingled with many great artists of the time, but ultimately shifted his ambitions toward writing, struggling to become a poet and playwright. Only after leaving Paris for London did Moore establish himself as a published writer, and in 1894, he found both critical praise and commercial success with his masterwork, the realist novel *Esther Waters*. He wrote about ten novels in addition to numerous essays and short stories before his death in 1933.

ALBERT NOBBS

by George Moore

Foreword by Glenn Close

PENGUIN BOOKS

PENGUIN BOOKS

Published by the Penguin Group
Penguin Group (USA) Inc., 375 Hudson Street, New York, New York
10014, U.S.A. • Penguin Group (Canada), 90 Eglinton Avenue East,
Suite 700, Toronto, Ontario, Canada M4P 2Y3 (a division of Pearson
Penguin Canada Inc.) • Penguin Books Ltd, 80 Strand, London WC2R
0RL, England • Penguin Ireland, 25 St Stephen's Green, Dublin 2,
Ireland (a division of Penguin Books Ltd) • Penguin Group (Australia),
250 Camberwell Road, Camberwell, Victoria 3124, Australia (a
division of Pearson Australia Group Pty Ltd) • Penguin Books India
Pvt Ltd, 11 Community Centre, Panchsheel Park, New Delhi – 110
017, India • Penguin Group (NZ), 67 Apollo Drive, Rosedale,
Auckland 0632, New Zealand (a division of Pearson New Zealand
Ltd) • Penguin Books (South Africa) (Pty) Ltd, 24 Sturdee Avenue,
Rosebank, Johannesburg 2196, South Africa

Penguin Books Ltd, Registered Offices:
80 Strand, London WC2R 0RL, England

"Albert Nobbs" first appeared in *A Story-Teller's Holiday* by George
Moore (1918). It was later published in *Celibate Lives* by George
Moore (1927).

This edition with a foreword by Glenn Close
first published in Penguin Books 2011

10 9 8 7 6 5 4 3 2 1

Foreword copyright © Glenn Close, 2011
All rights reserved

ISBN 978-0-14-312252-4

Thoughts of Albert Nobbs

Almost thirty years ago, I was introduced to the character Albert Nobbs. Simone Benmussa of the Theâtre Du Rond-Point in Paris had successfully mounted a stage adaptation of George Moore's novella in both Paris and London and was in New York to direct a production of the play, titled *The Singular Life of Albert Nobbs*, at the Manhattan Theatre Club. It was early in my career. I had just finished appearing in my first movie role—Jenny Fields in *The World According to Garp*. I remember that my audition for Ms. Benmussa was far from satisfactory. I was aware of the highly subtle complexity of Albert and found it incredibly challenging to try to play her in one five-minute scene.

So much so that I stopped in the middle of my audition and said, "I am not doing this character justice. I am boring myself, so I must be boring you. I'm sorry, but I think I'll go now." And I walked out. That evening, I heard from my agent that Simone thought my audition was the most interesting thing that had happened that day and wanted me to come back. I was thrilled, but determined to do better. So I contacted an acting coach whom I had heard about through friends, went in for a session with him, was able to get a bit more of a handle on Albert, went back to audition, and got the part. We had a successful run Off-Broadway, and then I went on to other things, having been cast in my second movie, *The Big Chill*.

The years went by. I was busy with my career, but the haunting character of Albert Nobbs never left me. In fact, she kept speaking to me, in her tentative, innocent manner, perched in her very own space in my heart. Albert was unforgettable because she embodies for me three human behaviors that I find deeply compelling: innocence, a lack of self-pity, and the capacity to be compelled by a dream.

Albert's innocence comes from the fact that she has never had any intimate relationships. Once she buries herself in the guise of a waiter, it is too dangerous for her to seek any human contact. In order to survive, she has to stay invisible. Because she is an innocent, Albert wields unconscious power. She does not judge her fellow man. Her face is like a mirror, causing people to react to her direct, unknowing gaze in ways that reveal, to themselves and to others, who they really are. Her innocence is also clownlike—the funny-tragic face of the human comedy in which we are all players.

Albert's lack of self-pity is due to the fact that she doesn't think the world owes her anything. She is thankful to have found a facade that enables her to have gainful employment in an age when nameless, penniless, unmarried women ended up as streetwalkers or in the poor house. She has worked hard and saved her money. She will never have to endure the shame and degradation of wretched poverty.

As a dreamer, ignorant of the fact that she lacks the tools to make her dream a reality, Albert gains our love and respect. I think all human beings are fed by dreams. We long to believe. We are moved by individuals who believe in something against the odds because nothing is easy for anyone and we want to believe that the impossible can, upon occasion, be possible.

Twenty-nine years after playing Albert on stage, I was able to play her in the film version of *Albert Nobbs*. She has stayed as intriguing and funny and heartbreaking as she was all those years ago. My journey began with the story that you are about to read. Be gentle with Albert. Learn from her, as I have, that to truly survive we all need to feel safe and have human connection. Like all of us, Albert deserves to be loved.

Glenn Close
New York City
November 2011

ALBERT
NOBBS

1

When we went up to Dublin in the 'sixties, Alec, we always put up at Morrison's Hotel, a big family hotel at the corner of Dawson Street, one that was well patronised by the gentry from all over Ireland, my father paying his bill every six months when he was able, which wasn't very often, for what with racing stables and elections following one after the other, Moore Hall wasn't what you'd call over-flowing with money. Now that I come to think of it, I can see Morrison's as clearly almost as I do Moore Hall: the front door opening into a short passage, with some half-dozen steps leading up into the house, the glass doors of the coffee-room showing through the dimness, and in front of the visitor a big staircase running up to the second landing. I remember long passages on the second landing, and half-way down these passages was the well. I don't know if it's right to speak of the well of a staircase, but I used to think of it as a well. It was always being drummed into me that I mustn't climb on to the banisters, a thing I wished to do, but was afraid to get astride of them, lest I should lose my head and fall all the way down to the ground floor. There was nothing to stop me from reaching it, if I lost my balance, except a few gas lamps. I think that both the long passages led to minor stairs, but I never followed either lest I should miss my way. A very big building was Morrison's Hotel, with passages running hither and thither, and little flights of stairs in all kinds of odd corners by which the visitors climbed to their apartments, and it needed all my attention to remember the way to our rooms on the second floor. We were always on the second floor in a big sitting-room overlooking College Green, and I remember the pair of windows, their lace curtains and their rep curtains, better than the passages, and better than the windows I can remember myself looking through the pane interested in the coal carts going by, the bell hitched on to the horse's collar jangling all the way down the street, the coalman himself sitting with his legs hanging over the shafts, driving from the wrong side and looking up at the windows to see if he could spy out an order. Fine horses were in these coal carts, stepping out as well as those in our own carriage.

I'm telling you these things for the pleasure of looking back and nothing else. I can see the sitting-room and myself as plainly as I can see the mountains beyond, in some ways plainer, and the waiter that used to attend on us, I can see him, though not as plainly as I see you, Alec; but I'm more knowledgeable of him, if you understand me rightly, and to this day I can recall the frights he gave me when he came behind me, awakening me from my dream of a coalman's life—what he said is forgotten, but his squeaky voice remains in my ears. He seemed to be always laughing at me, showing long, yellow teeth, and I used to be afraid to open the sitting-room door, for I'd be sure to find him waiting on the landing, his napkin thrown over his right shoulder. I think I was afraid he'd pick me up and kiss me. As the whole of my story is about him, perhaps I'd better describe him more fully, and to do that I will tell you that he was a tall, scraggy fellow, with big hips sticking out, and a long, thin throat. It was his throat that frightened me as much as anything about him, unless it was his nose, which was a great high one, or his melancholy eyes, which were pale blue and very small, deep in the head. He was old, but how old I cannot say, for everybody except children seems old to children. He was the ugliest thing I'd seen out of a fairy book, and I'd beg not to be left alone in the sitting room; and I'm sure I often asked my father and mother to take another set of rooms, which they never did, for they liked Albert Nobbs. And the guests liked him, and the proprietress liked him, as well she might, for he was the most dependable servant in the hotel; no running round to public-houses and coming back with the smell of whisky and tobacco upon him; no rank pipe in his pocket; and of all, no playing the fool with the maid-servants. Nobody had ever been heard to say he had seen Albert out with one of them—a queer, hobgoblin sort of fellow that they mightn't have cared to be seen with, but all the same it seemed to them funny that he should never propose to walk out with one of them. I've heard the hall-porter say it was hard to understand a man living without taking pleasure in something outside of his work. Holidays he never asked for, and when Mrs. Baker pressed him to go to the salt water for a week, he'd try to rake up an excuse for not going away, asking if it wasn't true that the Blakes, the Joyces, and the Ruttledges were coming up to town, saying that he didn't like to be away, so used were they to him and he to them. A strange life his was, and mysterious, though every hour of it was before them, saving the hours he was asleep, which weren't many, for he was no great sleeper. From the time he got up in the morning till he went to bed at night he was before their eyes, running up and down the staircase, his napkin over his arm, taking orders with cheerfulness, as if an order were as good as a half-crown tip to him, always good-humoured, and making amends for his lack of interest in other people by his willingness to oblige. No one had ever heard him object to doing anything he was asked to do, or even put forward an excuse for not being able to do it. In fact, his willingness to oblige was so notorious in the hotel that Mrs. Baker (the proprietress of Morrison's Hotel at the time) could hardly believe she was listening to him when he began to stumble from one excuse to another for not sharing his bed with Hubert Page, and this after she had told him that his bed was Page's only chance of getting a stretch that night. All the other waiters were married men and went home to their wives. You see, Alec, it was Punchestown week, and beds are as scarce in Dublin that week as diamonds are on the slopes of Croagh Patrick.

But you haven't told me yet who Page was, Alec interjected, and I thought reprovingly. I'm just coming to him, I answered. Hubert Page was a house-painter, well known and well liked by Mrs. Baker. He came over every season, and was always welcome at Morrison's Hotel, and so pleasant were his manners that one forgot the smell of his paint. It is hardly saying too much to say that when Hubert Page had finished his job everybody in the hotel, men and women alike, missed the pleasant sight of this young man going to and fro in his suit of hollands, the long coat buttoned loosely to his figure with large bone buttons, going to and fro about his work, up and down the passages, with a sort of lolling, idle gait that attracted and pleased the eye—a young man that would seem preferable to most men if a man had to choose a bed-fellow, yet seemingly the very one that Albert Nobbs couldn't abide lying down with, a dislike that Mrs. Baker could understand so little that she stood staring at her confused and embarrassed waiter, who was still seeking excuses for his dislike to share his bed with Hubert Page. I suppose you fully understand, she said, that Page is leaving for Belfast by the morning train, and has come over here to ask us for a bed, there not being one at the hotel in which he is working? Albert answered that he understood well enough, but was thinking— He began again to fumble with words. Now, what are you trying to say? Mrs. Baker asked, and rather sharply. My bed is full of lumps, Albert answered. Your mattress full of lumps! the proprietress rapped out; why, your mattress was repicked and buttoned six months ago, and came back as good as any mattress in the hotel. What kind of story are you telling me? So it was, ma'am, so it was, Albert mumbled, and it was some time before he got out his next excuse: he was a very light sleeper and had never slept with anybody before and was sure he wouldn't close his eyes; not that that would matter much, but his sleeplessness might keep Mr. Page awake. Mr. Page would get a better stretch on one of the sofas in the coffee-room than in my bed, I'm thinking, Mrs. Baker. A better stretch on the sofa in the coffee-room? Mrs. Baker repeated angrily. I don't understand you, not a little bit; and she stood staring at the two men, so dissimilar. But, ma'am, I wouldn't be putting Mr. Nobbs to the inconvenience of my company, the house-painter began. The night is a fine one; I'll keep myself warm with a sharp walk, and the train starts early. You'll do nothing of the kind, Page, she answered; and seeing that Mrs. Baker was now very angry, Albert thought it time to give in, and without more ado he began to assure them both that he'd be glad of Mr. Page's company in his bed. I should think so indeed! interjected Mrs. Baker. But I'm a light sleeper, he added. We've heard that before, Albert! Of course, if Mr. Page is pleased to share my bed, Albert continued, I shall be very glad. If Mr. Nobbs doesn't like my company I should— Don't say another word, Albert whispered, you'll only set her against me. Come upstairs at once; it'll be all right. Come along.

Good-night, ma'am, and I hope— No inconvenience whatever, Page, Mrs. Baker answered. This way, Mr. Page, Albert cried; and as soon as they were in the room he said: I hope you aren't going to cut up rough at anything I've said; it isn't at all as Mrs. Baker put it. I'm glad enough of your company, but you see, as I've never slept with anybody in my life, it may be that I shall be tossing about all night, keeping you awake. Well, if it's to be like that, Page answered, I might as well have a doze on the chair until it's time to go, and not trouble you at all. You won't be giving me any trouble; what I'm afraid of is—but enough has been said; we have to lie down together, whether we like it or whether we don't, for if Mrs. Baker heard that we hadn't been in the same bed together all the fault would lie with me. I'd be sent out of the hotel in double-quick time. But how can she know? Page cried. It's been settled one way, so let us make no more fuss about it.

Albert began to undo his white neck-tie, saying he would try to lie quiet, and Page started pulling off his clothes, thinking he'd be well pleased to be out of the job of lying down with Albert. But he was so dog-tired that he couldn't think any more about whom he was to sleep with, only of the long days of twelve and thirteen hours he had been doing, with a walk to and from his work; only sleep mattered to him, and Albert saw him tumble into bed in the long shirt that he wore under his clothes, and lay himself down next to the wall. It would be better for him to lie on the outside, Albert said to himself, but he didn't like to say anything lest Page might get out of his bed in a fit of ill-humour; but Page, as I've said, was too tired to trouble himself which side of the bed he was to doss on. A moment after he was asleep, and Albert stood listening, his loosened tie dangling, till the heavy breathing from the bed told him that Page was sound asleep. To make full sure he approached the bed stealthily, and overlooking Page, said: Poor fellow, I'm glad he's in my bed, for he'll get a good sleep there and he wants it; and considering that things had fallen out better than he hoped for, he began to undress.

* * *

He must have fallen asleep at once, and soundly, for he awoke out of nothingness. Flea! he muttered, and a strong one, too. It must have come from the housepainter alongside of me; a flea will leave anyone to come to me. And turning round in bed he remembered the look of dismay that had appeared on the housemaids' faces yesterday on his telling them that no man would ever love their hides as much as a flea loved his, which was so true that he couldn't understand how it was that the same flea had taken so long to find him out. Fleas must be as partial to him, he said, as they are to me. There it is again, trying to make up for lost time! and out went Albert's leg. I'm afraid I've awakened him, he said, but Hubert only turned over in the bed to sleep more soundly. It's a mercy indeed that he is so tired, Albert said, for if he wasn't very tired that last jump I gave would have awakened him. A moment after Albert was nipped again by another flea, or by the same one, he couldn't tell; he thought it must be a second one, so vigorous was the bite, and he was hard put to it to keep his nails off the spots. I shall only make them worse if I scratch, he said, and he strove to lie quiet. But the torment was too great. I've got to get up, he muttered, and raising himself up quietly, he listened. The striking of a match won't awaken him out of that sleep! and remembering where he had put the match-box, his hand was on it at once. The match flared up; he lighted the candle, and stood a while overlooking his bed-fellow. I'm safe, he said, and set himself to the task of catching the flea. There he is on the tail of my shirt, hardly able to move with all the blood he's taken from me. Now for the soap; and as he was about to dab it upon the blood-filled insect the painter awoke with a great yawn, and turning round, he said: Lord amassy! what is the meaning of this? Why, you're a woman!

If Albert had had the presence of mind to drop her shirt over her shoulders and to answer: You're dreaming, my man, Page might have turned over and fallen asleep and in the morning forgotten all about it, or thought he had been dreaming. But Albert hadn't a word in her chops. At last she began to blub. You won't tell on me, and ruin a poor man, will you, Mr. Page? That is all I ask of you, and on my knees I beg it. Get up from your knees, my good woman, said Hubert. My good woman! Albert repeated, for she had been about so long as a man that she only remembered occasionally that she was a woman. My good woman, Hubert repeated, get up from your knees and tell me how long you have been playing this part. Ever since I was a girl, Albert answered. You won't tell upon me, will you, Mr. Page, and prevent a poor woman from getting her living? Not likely, I've no thought of telling on you, but I'd like to hear how it all came about. How I went out as a youth to get my living? Yes; tell me the story, Hubert answered, for though I was very sleepy just now, the sleep has left my eyes and I'd like to hear it. But before you begin, tell me what you were doing with your shirt off. A flea, Albert answered. I suffer terribly from fleas, you must have brought some in with you, Mr. Page. I shall be covered in blotches in the morning. I'm sorry for that, Hubert said; but tell me how long ago it was that you became a man. Before you came to Dublin, of course? Oh, yes, long before. It is very cold, she said, and shuddering, dropped her shirt over her shoulders and pulled on her trousers.

2

It was in London, soon after the death of my old nurse, she began. You know I'm not Irish, Mr. Page. My parents may have been, for all I know. The only one who knew who they were was my old nurse, and she never told me. Never told you! interjected Hubert. No, she never told me, though I often asked her, saying no good could come of holding it back from me. She might have told me before she died, but she died suddenly. Died suddenly, Hubert repeated, without telling you who you were! You'd better begin at the beginning.

I don't know how I'm to do that, for the story seems to me to be without a beginning; anyway I don't know the beginning. I was a bastard, and no one but my old nurse, who brought me up, knew who I was; she said she'd tell me some day, and she hinted more than once that my people were grand folk, and I know she had a big allowance from them for my education. Whoever they were, a hundred a year was paid to her for my keep and education, and all went well with us so long as my parents lived, but when they died the allowance was no longer paid, and my nurse and myself had to go out to work. It was all very sudden: one day the Reverend Mother (I got my education at a convent school) told me that Mrs. Nobbs, my old nurse; had sent for me, and the first news I had on coming home was that my parents were dead and that we'd have to get our own living henceforth. There was no time for picking and choosing. We hadn't what would keep us until the end of the month in the house, so out we had to go in search of work; and the first job that came our way was looking after chambers in the Temple. We had three gentlemen to look after, so there was eighteen shillings a week between my old nurse and myself; the omnibus fares had to come out of these wages, and to save sixpence a day we went to live in Temple Lane. My old nurse didn't mind the lane; she had been a working woman all her life; but with me it was different, and the change was so great from the convent that I often thought I would sooner die than continue to live amid rough people. There was nothing wrong with them; they were honest enough; but they were poor, and when you are very poor you live like the animals, indecently, and life without decency is hardly bearable, so I thought. I've been through a great deal since in different hotels, and have become used to hard work, but even now I can't think of Temple Lane without goose-flesh; and when Mrs. Nobbs's brother lost his berth (he'd been a bandmaster, a bugler, or something to do with music in the country), my old nurse was obliged to give him sixpence a day, and the drop from eighteen shillings to fourteen and sixpence is a big one. My old nurse worried about the food, but it was the rough men I worried about; the bandsman wouldn't leave me alone, and many's the time I've waited until the staircase was clear, afraid that if I met him or another that I'd be caught hold of and held and pulled about. I was different then from what I am now, and might have been tempted if one of them had been less rough than the rest, and if I hadn't known I was a bastard; it was that, I think, that kept me straight more than anything else, for I had just begun to feel what a great misfortune it is for a poor girl to find herself in the family way; no greater misfortune can befall anyone in this world, but it would have been worse in my case, for I should have known that I was only bringing another bastard into the world.

I escaped being seduced in the lane, and in the chambers the barristers had their own mistresses; pleasant and considerate men they all were— pleasant to work for; and it wasn't until four o'clock came and our work was over for the day that my heart sank, for after four o'clock till we went to bed at night there was nothing for us to do but to listen to the screams of drunken women; I don't know which was the worser, the laughter or the curses.

One of the barristers we worked for was Mr. Congreve; he had chambers in Temple Gardens overlooking the river, and it was a pleasure to us to keep his pretty things clean, never breaking one of them; it was a pleasure for my old nurse as well as myself, myself more than for her, for though I wasn't very sure of myself at the time, looking back now I can see that I must have loved Mr. Congreve very dearly; and it couldn't be else, for I had come out of a convent of nuns where I had been given a good education, where all was good, quiet, refined and gentle, and Mr. Congreve seemed in many ways to remind me of the convent, for he never missed Church; as rare for him to miss a service as for parson. There was plenty of books in his chambers and he'd lend them to me, and talk to me over his newspaper when I took in his breakfast, and ask about the convent and what the nuns were like, and I'd stand in front of him, my eyes fixed on him, not feeling the time going by. I can see him now as plainly as if he were before me—very thin and elegant, with long white hands, and beautifully dressed. Even in the old clothes that he wore of a morning there wasn't much fault to find; he wore old clothes more elegantly than any man in the Temple wore his new clothes. I used to know all his suits, as well I might, for it was my job to look after them, to brush them; and I used to spend a

great deal more time than was needed taking out
spots with benzine, arranging his neck-ties he had
fifty or sixty, all kinds—and seven or eight great-
coats. A real toff—my word he was that, but not
one of those haughty ones too proud to give one a
nod. He always smiled and nodded if we met under
the clock, he on his way to the library and I returning to Temple Lane. I used to look round after him
saying: He's got on the striped trousers and the
embroidered waistcoat. Mr. Congreve was a com-
pensation for Temple Lane; he had promised to
take me into his private service, and I was counting
the days when I should leave Temple Lane, when
one day I said to myself: Why, here's a letter from a
woman. You see, Mr. Congreve wasn't like the
other young men in the Temple; I never found a
hairpin in his bed, and if I had I shouldn't have
thought as much of him as I did. Nice is in France,
I said, and thought no more about the matter until
another letter arrived from Nice. Now what can
she be writing to him about? I asked, and thought
no more about it until the third letter arrived. Yesterday is already more than half forgotten, but the
morning I took in that last letter is always before

me. And it was a few mornings afterwards that a box of flowers came for him. A parcel for you, sir, I said. He roused himself up in bed. For me? he cried, putting out his hand, and the moment he saw the writing, he said: Put the flowers in water. He knows all about it, I said to myself, and so overcome was I as I picked them up out of the box that a sudden faintness came over me, and my old nurse said: What is the matter with thee? She never guessed, and I couldn't have told her if I had wished to, for at the time it was no more than a feeling that so far as I was concerned all was over. Of course I never thought that Mr. Congreve would look at me, and I don't know that I wanted him to, but I didn't want another woman about the place, and I seemed to know from that moment what was going to happen. She isn't far away now, in the train maybe, I said, as I went about my work, and these rooms will be mine no longer. Of course they never were mine; but you know what I mean.

A week later he said to me: There's a lady coming to luncheon here, and I remember the piercing that the words caused me; I can feel them here still; and Albert put her hand to her heart. Well, I had to serve the luncheon, working round the table and they not minding me at all, but sitting looking at each other lost in a sense of delight; the luncheon was forgotten. They don't want me waiting about, I thought. I knew all this, and said to myself in the kitchen: It's disgraceful, it's wicked, to lead a man into sin—for all my anger went out against the woman, and not against Mr. Congreve; in my eyes he seemed to be nothing more than a victim of a designing woman; that is how I looked at it at the time, being but a youngster only just come from a convent school.

I don't think that anyone suffered more than I did in those days. It all seems very silly now when I look back upon it, but it was very real then. It does seem silly to tell that I used to lie awake all night thinking to myself that Mr. Congreve was an elegant gentleman and I but a poor serving girl that he'd never look twice at, thinking of her only as somebody to go to the cellar for coal or to the kitchen to fetch his breakfast. I don't think I ever hoped he'd fall in love with me. It wasn't as bad as that. It was the hopelessness of it that set the tears streaming down my cheeks over my pillow, and I used to stuff the sheet into my mouth to keep back the sobs lest my old nurse should hear me; it wouldn't do to keep her awake, for she was very ill at that time; and soon afterward she died, and then I was left alone, without a friend in the world. The only people I knew were the charwomen that lived in Temple Lane, and the bugler, who began to bully me, saying that I must continue to give him the same money he had had from my old nurse. He caught me on the stairs once and twisted my arm until I thought he'd broken it. The month after my old nurse's death till I went to earn my living as a waiter was the hardest time of all, and Mr. Congreve's kindness seemed to hurt me more than anything. If only he'd spared me his kind words, and not spoken about the extra money he was going to give me for my attendance on his lady, I shouldn't have felt so much that they had lain side by side in the bed that I was making. She brought a dressing-gown to the chambers and some slippers, and then more luggage came along; and I think she must have guessed I was in love with Mr. Congreve, for I heard them quarrelling—my name was mentioned; and I said: I can't put up with it any longer;

whatever the next life may be like, it can't be worse than this one for me at least; and as I went to and fro between Temple Lane and the chambers in Temple Gardens I began to think how I might make away with myself. I don't know if you know London, Hubert? Yes, he said; I'm a Londoner, but I come here to work every year. Then if you know the Temple, you know that the windows of Temple Gardens overlook the river. I used to stand at those windows watching the big brown river flowing through its bridges, thinking all the while of the sea into which it went, and that I must plunge into the river and be carried away down to the sea, or be picked up before I got there. I could only think about making an end to my trouble and of the Frenchwoman. Her suspicions that I cared for him made her harder on me than she need have been; she was always coming the missis over me. Her airs and graces stiffened my back more than anything else, and I'm sure if I hadn't met Bessie Lawrence I should have done away with myself. She was the woman who used to look after the chambers under Mr. Congreve's. We stopped talking outside the gateway by King's Bench Walk—if you know the Temple, you know where I mean. Bessie kept talking, but I wasn't listening, only catching a word here and there, not waking up from the dream how to make away with myself till I heard the words: If I had a figure like yours. As no one had ever spoken about my figure before, I said: Now what has my figure got to do with it? You haven't been listening to me, she said, and I answered that I had only missed the last few words. Just missed the last few words, she said testily; you didn't hear me telling you that there is a big dinner at the Freemason's Tavern tonight, and they're short of waiters. But what has that got to do with my figure? I asked. That shows, she rapped out, that you haven't been listening to me. Didn't I say that if it wasn't for my hips and bosom I'd very soon be into a suit of evening clothes and getting ten shillings for the job. But what has that got to do with my figure? I repeated. Your figure is just the one for a waiter's. Oh, I'd never thought of that, says I, and we said no more. But the words: Your figure is just the one for a waiter's, kept on in my head till my eyes caught sight of a bundle of old clothes that Mr. Congreve had given me to sell.

A suit of evening clothes was in it. You see, Mr. Congreve and myself were about the same height and build. The trousers will want a bit of shortening, I said to myself, and I set to work; and at six o'clock I was in them and down at the Freemason's Tavern answering questions, saying that I had been accustomed to waiting at table. All the waiting I had done was bringing in Mr. Congreve's dinner from the kitchen to the sitting-room: a roast chicken or a chop, and in my fancy it seemed to me that the waiting at the Freemason's Tavern would be much the same. The head waiter looked me over a bit doubtfully and asked if I had had experience with public dinners. I thought he was going to turn me down, but they were short-handed, so I was taken on, and it was a mess that I made of it, getting in everybody's way; but my awkwardness was taken in good part and I received ten shillings, which was good money for the sort of work I did that night. But what stood to me was not so much the ten shillings that I earned as the bit I had learned. It was only a bit, not much bigger than a threepenny bit; but I had worked round a table at a big dinner, and feeling certain that I could learn what I didn't know, I asked for another job. I suppose the head waiter could see that there was the making of a waiter in me, for on coming out of the Freemason's Tavern he stopped me to ask if I was going back to private service as soon as I could get a place. The food I'd had and the excitement of the dinner, the guests, the lights, the talk, stood to me, and things seemed clearer than they had ever seemed before. My feet were of the same mind, for they wouldn't walk towards the Temple, and I answered the head waiter that I'd be glad of another job. Well, said he, you don't much know about the work, but you're an honest lad, I think, so I'll see what I can do for you; and at the moment a thought struck him. Just take this letter, said he, to the Holborn Restaurant. There's a dinner there and I've had word that they're short of a waiter or two. Be off as fast as you can. And away I went as fast as my legs could carry me, and they took me there in good time, in front, by a few seconds, of two other fellows who were after the job. I got it. Another job came along, and another and another. Each of them jobs was worth ten shillings to me, to say nothing of the learning of the trade; and having, as I've said, the making of a waiter in me, it didn't take more than about three months for me to be as quick and as smart and as watchful as the best of them, and without them qualities no one will succeed in waiting. I have worked round the tables in the biggest places in London and all over England in all the big towns, in Manchester, in Liverpool, and Birmingham; I am well known at the old Hen and Chickens, at the Queen's, and the Plough and Harrow in Birmingham. It was seven years ago that I came here, and here it would seem that I've come to be looked on as a fixture, for the Bakers are good people to work for and I didn't like to leave them when, three years ago, a good place was offered to me, so kind were they to me in my illness. I suppose one never remains always in the same place, but I may as well be here as elsewhere.

Seven years working in Morrison's Hotel, Page said, and on the second floor? Yes, the second floor is the best in the hotel; the money is better than in the coffee room, and that is why the Bakers have put me here, Albert replied. I wouldn't care to leave them; they've often said they don't know what they'd do without me. Seven years, Hubert repeated, the same work up the stairs and down the stairs, banging into the kitchen and out again. There's more variety in the work than you think for, Hubert, Albert answered. Every family is different, and so you're always learning. Seven years, Page repeated, neither man nor woman, just a perhapser. He spoke these words more to himself than to Nobbs, but feeling he had expressed himself incautiously he raised his eyes and read on Albert's face that the words had gone home, and that this outcast from both sexes felt her loneliness perhaps more keenly than before. As Hubert was thinking what words he might use to conciliate Albert with her lot, Albert repeated the words: Neither man nor woman; yet nobody ever suspected, she muttered, and never would have suspected me till the day of my death if it hadn't been for that flea that you brought in with you. But what harm did the flea do? I'm bitten all over, said Albert, scratching her thighs. Never mind the bites, said Hubert; we wouldn't have had this talk if it hadn't been for the flea, and I shouldn't have heard your story.

Tears trembled on Albert's eyelids; she tried to

keep them back, but they overflowed the lids and were soon running quickly down her cheeks. You've heard my story, she said. I thought nobody would ever hear it, and I thought I should never cry again; and Hubert watched the gaunt woman shaking with sobs under a coarse nightshirt. It's all much sadder than I thought it was, and if I'd known how sad it was I shouldn't have been able to live through it. But I've jostled along somehow, she added, always merry and bright, with never anyone to speak to, not really to speak to, only to ask for plates and dishes, for knives and forks and such like, tablecloths and napkins, cursing betimes the life you've been through; for the feeling cannot help coming over us, perhaps over the biggest as over the smallest, that all our trouble is for nothing and can end in nothing. It might have been better if I had taken the plunge. But why am I thinking these things? It's you that has set me thinking, Hubert. I'm sorry if— Oh, it's no use being sorry, and I'm a great silly to cry like this. I thought that regrets had passed away with the petticoats. But you've awakened the woman in me. You've brought it all up again. But I mustn't let on like this; it's very foolish of an old perhapser like me, neither man nor woman! But I can't help it. She began to sob again, and in the midst of her grief the word loneliness was uttered, and when the paroxysm was over, Hubert said: Lonely, yes, I suppose it is lonely; and he put his hand out towards Albert. You're very good, Mr. Page, and I'm sure you'll keep my secret, though indeed I don't care very much whether you do or not. Now, don't let on like that again, Hubert said. Let us have a little chat and try to understand each other. I'm sure it's lonely for you to live without man or without woman, thinking like a man and feeling like a woman. You seem to know all about it, Hubert. I hadn't thought of it like that before myself, but when you speak the words I feel you have spoken the truth. I suppose I was wrong to put off my petticoats and step into those trousers. I wouldn't go so far as to say that, Hubert answered, and the words were so unexpected that Albert forgot her grief for a moment and said: Why do you say that, Hubert? Well, because I was thinking, he replied, that you might marry. But I was never a success as a girl. Men didn't look at me then, so I'm sure they wouldn't now I'm a middle-aged woman. Marriage! whom should I marry? No, there's no marriage for me in the world; I must go on being a man. But you won't tell on me? You've promised, Hubert. Of course I won't tell, but I don't see why you shouldn't marry. What do you mean, Hubert? You aren't putting a joke upon me, are you? If you are it's very unkind. A joke upon you? no, Hubert answered. I didn't mean that you should marry a man, but you might marry a girl. Marry a girl? Albert repeated, her eyes wide open and staring. A girl? Well, anyway, that's what I've done, Hubert replied. But you're a young man and a very handsome young man too. Any girl would like to have you, and I dare say they were all after you before you met the right girl. I'm not a young man, I'm a woman, Hubert replied. Now I know for certain, cried Albert, you're putting a joke upon me. A woman! Yes, a woman; you can feel for yourself if you won't be-lieve me. Put your hand under my shirt; you'll find nothing there. Albert moved away instinctively, her modesty having been shocked. You see I offered myself like that feeling you couldn't take my word for it. It isn't a thing there can be any doubt about. Oh, I believe you, Albert replied. And now that that matter is settled, Hubert began, perhaps you'd like to hear my story; and without waiting for an answer she related the story of her unhappy marriage: her husband, a house-painter, had changed towards her altogether after the birth of her second child, leaving her without money for food and selling up the home twice. At last I decided to have another cut at it, Hubert went on, and catching sight of my husband's working clothes one day I said to myself: He's often made me put these on and go out and help him with his job; why shouldn't I put them on for myself and go away for good? I didn't like leaving the children, but I couldn't remain with him. But the marriage? Albert asked. It was lonely going home to an empty room; I was as lonely as you, and one day, meeting a girl as lonely as myself, I said: Come along, and we arranged to live together, each paying our share. She had her work and I had mine, and between us we made a fair living; and this I can say with truth, that we haven't known an unhappy hour since we married. People began to talk, so we had to. I'd like you to see our home. I always return to my home after a job is finished with a light heart and leave it with a heavy one. But I don't understand, Albert said. What don't you understand? Hubert asked. Whatever Albert's thoughts were, they faded from her, and her eyelids dropped over her eyes. You're falling asleep, Hubert said, and I'm doing the same. It must be three o'clock in the morning and I've to catch the five o'clock train. I can't think now of what I was going to ask you, Albert muttered, but you'll tell me in the morning; and turning over, she made a place for Hubert.

3

What has become of him? Albert said, rousing herself, and then, remembering that Hubert's intention
was to catch the early train, she began to remember. His train, she said, started from Amiens Street
at—I must have slept heavily for him—for her not
to have awakened me, or she must have stolen
away very quietly. But, lord amassy, what time is
it? And seeing she had overslept herself a full hour,
she began to dress herself, muttering all the while:
Such a thing never happened to me before. And the
hotel as full as it can hold. Why didn't they send
for me? The missis had a thought of my bedfellow,
mayhap, and let me sleep it out. I told her I
shouldn't close an eye till she left me. But I mustn't

fall into the habit of sheing him. Lord, if the missis knew everything! But I've overslept myself a full hour, and if nobody has been up before somebody soon will be. The greater haste the less speed. All the same, despite the difficulty of finding her clothes, Albert was at work on her landing some twenty minutes after, running up and down the stairs, preparing for the different breakfasts in the half-dozen sitting-rooms given to her charge, driving everybody before her, saying: We're late today, and the house full of visitors. How is it that 54 isn't turned out? Has 35 rung his bell? Lord, Albert, said a housemaid, I wouldn't worry my fat because I was down late; once in a way don't hurt. And sitting up half the night talking to Mr. Page, said another maid, and then rounding on us. Half the night talking, Albert repeated. My bed-fellow! Where is Mr. Page? I didn't hear him go away; he may have missed his train for aught I know. But do you be getting on with your work, and let me be getting on with mine. You're very cross this morning, Albert, the maid-servant muttered, and retired to chatter with two other maids who were looking over the banisters at the time.

Well, Mr. Nobbs, the head porter began, when Albert came running downstairs to see some visitors off, and to receive her tips—well, Mr. Nobbs, how did you find your bed-fellow? Oh, he was all right, but I'm not used to bed-fellows, and he brought a flea with him, and it kept me awake; and when I did fall asleep, I slept so heavily that I was an hour late. I hope he caught his train. But what is all this pother about bed-fellows? Albert asked herself, as she returned to her landing. Page hasn't said anything, no, she's said nothing, for we are both in the same boat, and to tell on me would be to tell on herself. I'd never have believed if— Albert's modesty prevented her from finishing the sentence. She's a woman right enough. But the cheek of it, to marry an innocent girl! Did she let the girl into the secret, or leave her to find it out when— The girl might have called in the police! This was a question one might ponder on, and by luncheon time Albert was inclined to believe that Hubert told his wife before— She couldn't have had the cheek to wed her, Albert said, without warning her that things might not turn out as she fancied. Mayhap, Albert continued, she didn't tell her before they wedded and mayhap she did, and being one of them like myself that isn't always hankering after a man she was glad to live with Hubert for companionship. Albert tried to remember the exact words that Hubert had used. It seemed to her that Hubert had said that she lived with a girl first and wedded her to put a stop to people's scandal. Of course they could hardly live together except as man and wife. She remembered Hubert saying that she always returned home with a light heart and never left it without a heavy one. So it would seem that this marriage was as successful as any and a great deal more than most.

At that moment 35 rang his bell. Albert hurried to answer it, and it was not till late in the evening, between nine and ten o'clock, when the guests were away at the theatres and concerts and nobody was about but two maids, that Albert, with her napkin over her shoulder, dozed and meditated on the advice that Hubert had given her. She should marry, Hubert had said; Hubert had married. Of course it wasn't a real marriage, it couldn't be that, but a very happy one it would seem. But the girl must have understood that she was not marrying a man. Did Hubert tell her before wedding her or after, and what were the words? She would have liked to know the words: For after all I've worked hard, she said, and her thoughts melted away into meditation of what her life had been for the last five-and-twenty years, a mere drifting, it seemed to her, from one hotel to another, without friends; meeting, it is true, sometimes men and women who seemed willing to be friendly. But her secret forced her to live apart from men as well as women; the clothes she wore smothered the woman in her; she no longer thought and felt as she used to when she wore petticoats, and she didn't think and feel like a man though she wore trousers. What was she? Nothing, neither man nor woman, so small wonder she was lonely. But Hubert had put off her sex, so she said. . . . Albert turned over in her mind the possibility that a joke had been put upon her, and fell to thinking what Hubert's home might be like, and was vexed with herself for not having asked if she had a clock and vases an the chimney-piece. One of the maids called from the end of the passage, and when Albert received 54's order and executed it, she returned to her seat in the passage, her napkin over her shoulder, and resumed her reverie. It seemed to her that Hubert once said that her wife was a milliner; Hubert may not have spoken the word milliner; but if she hadn't it was strange that the word should keep on coming up in her mind. There was no reason why the wife shouldn't be a milliner, and if that were, so it was as likely as not that they owned a house in some quiet, insignificant street, letting the dining-room, back room and kitchen to a widow or to a pair of widows. The drawing-room was the workroom and showroom; Page and his wife slept in the room above. On second thoughts it seemed to Albert that if the business were millinery it might be that Mrs. Page would prefer the ground floor for her showroom. A third and fourth distribution of the "premises" presented itself to Albert's imagination. On thinking the matter over again it seemed to her that Hubert did not speak of a millinery business but of a seamstress, and if that were so, a small dressmaker's business in a quiet street would be in keeping with all Hubert had said about the home. Albert was not sure, however, that if she found a girl willing to share her life with her, it would be a seamstress's business she would be on the look-out for. She thought that a sweetmeat shop, newspapers and tobacco, would be her choice.

Why shouldn't she make a fresh start? Hubert had no difficulties. She had said—Albert could recall the very words—I didn't mean you should marry a man, but a girl. Albert had saved, oh! how she had tried to save, for she didn't wish to end her days in the workhouse. She had saved upwards of five hundred pounds, which was enough to purchase a little business, and her heart dilated as she thought of her two successful investments in house property. In six months' time she hoped to have six hundred pounds, and if it took her two years to find a partner and a business, she would have at least seventy or eighty pounds more, which would be a great help, for it would be a mistake to put one's money into a falling business. If she found a partner, she'd have to do like Hubert; for marriage would put a stop to all tittle-tattle; she'd be able to keep her place at Morrison's Hotel, or perhaps leave Morrison's and rely on jobs; and with her connection it would be a case of picking and choosing the best: ten and sixpence a night, nothing under. She dreamed of a round. Belfast, Liverpool, Manchester, Bradford, rose up in her imagination, and after a month's absence, a couple of months maybe, she would return home, her heart anticipating a welcome—a real welcome, for though she would continue to be a man to the world, she would be a woman to the dear one at home. With a real partner, one whose heart was in the business, they might make as much as two hundred pounds a year—four pounds a week! And with four pounds a week their home would be as pretty and happy as any in the city of Dublin. Two rooms and a kitchen were what she foresaw. The furniture began to creep into her imagination little by little. A large sofa by the fireplace covered with a chintz! But chintz dirtied quickly in the city; a dark velvet sofa might be more suitable. It would cost a great deal of money, five or six pounds; and at that rate fifty pounds wouldn't go very far, for they must have a fine double-bed mattress; and if they were going to do things in that style, the home would cost them eighty pounds. With luck these eighty pounds could be earned within the next two years at Morrison's Hotel.

Albert ran over in her mind the tips she had received. The people in 34 were leaving tomorrow; they were always good for half a sovereign, and she decided then and there that tomorrow's half-sovereign must be put aside as a beginning of a sum of money for the purchase of a clock to stand on a marble chimney-piece or a mahogany chiffonier. A few days after she got a sovereign from a departing guest, and it revealed a pair of pretty candlesticks and a round mirror. Her tips were no longer mere white and yellow metal stamped with the effigy of a dead king or a living queen, but symbols of the future that awaited her. An unexpected crown set her pondering on the colour of the curtains in their sitting-room, and Albert became suddenly conscious that a change had come into her life: the show was the same—carrying plates and dishes upstairs and downstairs, and taking orders for drinks and cigars; but behind the show a new life was springing up—a life strangely personal and associated with the life without only in this much, that the life without was now a vassal state paying tribute to the life within. She wasn't as good a servant as heretofore. She knew it. Certain absences of mind, that was all; and the servants as they went by with their dusters began to wonder whatever Albert could be dreaming of.

It was about this time that the furnishing of the parlour at the back of the shop was completed, likewise that of the bedroom above the shop, and Albert had just entered on another dream—a dream of a shop with two counters, one at which cigars, tobacco, pipes and matches were sold, and at the other all kinds of sweetmeats, a shop with a door leading to her wife's parlour. A changing figure the wife was in Albert's imagination, turning from fair to dark, from plump to slender, but capturing her imagination equally in all her changes; sometimes she was accompanied by a child of three or four, a boy, the son of a dead man, for in one of her dreams Albert married a widow. In another and more frequent dream she married a woman who had transgressed the moral code and been deserted before the birth of her child. In this case it would be supposed that Albert had done the right thing, for after leading the girl astray he had made an honest woman of her. Albert would be the father in everybody's eyes except the mother's, and she hoped that the child's mother would outgrow all the memory of the accidental seed sown, as the saying runs, in a foolish five minutes. A child would be a pleasure to them both, and a girl in the family way appealed to her more than a widow; a girl that some soldier, the boot-boy, or the hotel porter, had gotten into trouble; and Albert kept her eyes and ears open, hoping to rescue from her precarious situation one of those unhappy girls that were always cropping up in Morrison's Hotel. Several had had to leave the hotel last year, but not one this year. But some revivalist meetings were going to be held in Dublin. Many of our girls attend them, and an unlucky girl will be in luck's way if we should run across one another. Her thought passed into a dream of the babe that would come into the world some three or four months after their marriage, her little soft hands and expressive eyes claiming their protection, asking for it. What matter whether she calls me father or mother? They are but mere words that the lips speak, but love is in the heart and only love matters.

* * *

Now whatever can Albert be brooding? an idle housemaid asked herself as she went by. Brooding a love story? Not likely. A marriage with some girl outside? He isn't over-partial to any of us. That Albert was brooding something, that there was something on his mind, became the talk of the hotel, and soon after it came to be noticed that Albert was eager to avail himself of every excuse to absent himself from duty in the hotel. He had been seen in the smaller streets looking up at the houses. He had saved a good deal of money, and some of his savings were invested in house property, so it was possible that his presence in these streets might be explained by the supposition that he was investing new sums of money in house property, or, and it was the second suggestion that stimulated the imagination, that Albert was going to be married and was looking out for a house for his wife. He had been seen talking with Annie Watts; but she was not in the family way after all, and despite her wistful eyes and gentle voice she was not chosen. Her heart is not in her work, Albert said; she thinks only of when she can get out, and that isn't the sort for a shop, whereas Dorothy Keyes is a glutton for work; but Albert couldn't abide the tall, angular woman, built like a boy, with a neck like a swan's. Besides her unattractive appearance, her manner was abrupt. But Alice's small, neat figure and quick intelligence marked her out for the job. Alas! Alice was hot-tempered. We should quarrel, Albert said, and picking up her napkin, which had slipped from her knee to the floor, she considered the maids on the floor above. A certain stateliness of figure and also of gait put the thought into her mind that Mary O'Brien would make an attractive shopwoman. But her second thoughts were that Mary O'Brien was a Papist, and the experience of Irish Protestants shows that Papists and Protestants don't mix.

She had just begun to consider the next housemaid, when a voice interrupted her musing. That lazy girl, Annie Watts, on the look-out for an excuse to chatter the time away instead of being about her work, were the words that crossed Albert's mind as she raised her eyes, and so unwelcoming were they that Annie in her nervousness began to hesitate and stammer, unable for the moment to find a subject, plunging at last, and rather awkwardly, into the news of the arrival of the new kitchen-maid, Helen Dawes, but never dreaming that the news could have any interest for Albert. To her surprise, Albert's eyes lighted up. Do you know her? Annie asked. Know her? Albert answered. No, I don't know her, but— At that moment a bell rang. Oh, bother, Annie said, and while she moved away idling along the banisters, Albert hurried down the passage to enquire what No. 47 wanted, and to learn that he needed writing-paper and envelopes. He couldn't write with the pens the hotel furnished; would Albert be so kind as to ask the page-boy to fetch some J's? With pleasure, Albert said; with pleasure. Would you like to have the writing-paper and envelopes before the boy returns with the pens, sir? The visitor answered that the writing-paper and envelopes would be of no use to him till he had gotten the pens. With pleasure, sir; with pleasure; and whilst waiting for the page to return she passed through the swing doors and searched for a new face among the different young women passing to and fro between

the white-aproned and white-capped chefs, bringing the dishes to the great zinc counter that divided
the kitchen-maids and the scullions from the waiters. She must be here, she said, and returned again
to the kitchen in the hope of meeting the new-
comer, Helen Dawes, who, when she was found,
proved to be very unlike the Helen Dawes of Albert's imagination. A thick-set, almost swarthy girl
of three-and-twenty, rather under than above the
medium height, with white, even teeth, but unfor-
tunately protruding, giving her the appearance of a
rabbit. Her eyes seemed to be dark brown, but on
looking into them Albert discovered them to be
grey-green, round eyes that dilated and flashed
wonderfully while she talked. Her face lighted up;
and there was a vindictiveness in her voice that
appeared and disappeared; Albert suspected her,
and was at once frightened and attracted. Vindictiveness in her voice! How could such a thing have
come into my mind? she said a few days after. A
more kindly girl it would be difficult to find. How
could I have been so stupid? She is one of those,
Albert continued, that will be a success in everything she undertakes; and dreams began soon after

that the sweetstuff and tobacco shop could hardly fail to prosper under her direction. Nobody could befool Helen, and when I am away at work I shall feel certain that everything will be all right at home. It's a pity that she isn't in the family way, for it would be pleasant to have a little one running about the shop asking for lemon drops and to hear him calling us father and mother. At that moment a strange thought flitted across Albert's mind—after all, it wouldn't matter much to her if Helen were to get into the family way later; of course, there would be the expense of the lying-in. Her second thoughts were that women live happily enough till a man comes between them, and that it would be safer for her to forgo a child and choose an older woman. All the same, she could not keep herself from asking Helen to walk out with her, and the next time they met the words slipped out of her mouth: I shall be off duty at three today, and if you are not engaged— I am off duty at three, Helen answered. Are you engaged? Albert asked. Helen hesitated, it being the truth that she had been and was still walking out with one of the scullions, and was not sure he would look upon her going out with another, even though that one was such a harmless fellow as Albert Nobbs. Harmless in himself, she thought, and with a very good smell of money rising out of his pockets, very different from Joe, who seldom had a train fare upon him. But she hankered after Joe, and wouldn't give Albert a promise until she had asked him. Wants to walk out with you? Why, he has never been known to walk out with man, woman or child before. Well, that's a good one! I'd like to know what he's after, but I'm not jealous; you can go with him, there's no harm in Albert. I'm on duty: just go for a turn with him. Poke him up and see what he's after, and take him into a sweetshop and bring back a box of chocolates. Do you like chocolates? Helen asked, and her eyes flashing, she stood looking at Joe, who, thinking that her temper was rising, and wishing to quell it, asked hurriedly where she was going to meet him. At the corner, she answered. He is there already. Then be off, he said, and his tone grated. You wouldn't like me to keep him waiting? Helen said. Oh, dear no, not for Joe, not for Joseph, if he knows it, the scullion replied, lilting the song.

Helen turned away hoping that none of the maids would peach upon her, and Albert's heart rejoiced at seeing her on the other side of the street waiting for the tram to go by before she crossed it. Were you afraid I wasn't coming? she asked, and Albert, not being ready with words, answered shyly: Not very. A stupid answer this seemed to be to Helen, and it was in the hope of shuffling out of a tiresome silence that Albert asked her if she liked chocolates. Something under the tooth will help the time away, was the answer she got; and they went in search of a sweetmeat shop, Albert thinking that a shilling or one and sixpence would see her through it. But in a moment Helen's eyes were all over the shop, and spying out some large pictured boxes, she asked Albert if she might have one, and it being their first day out, Albert answered: Yes; but could not keep back the words: I'm afraid they'd cost a lot. For these words Albert got a contemptuous look, and Helen shook her shoulders so disdainfully that Albert pressed a second box on Helen—one to pass the time with, another to take home. To such a show of goodwill Helen felt she must respond, and her tongue rattled on pleasantly as she walked, crunching the chocolates, two between each lamp-post, Albert stinting herself to one, which she sucked slowly, hardly enjoying it at all, so worried was she by the loss of three and sixpence. As if Helen guessed the cause of Albert's disquiet, she called on her suitor to admire the damsel on the box, but Albert could not disengage her thoughts sufficiently from Helen's expensive tastes. If every walk were to cost three and sixpence there wouldn't be a lot left for the home in six months' time. And she fell to calculating how much it would cost her if they were to walk out once a week. Three fours are twelve and four sixpences are two shillings, fourteen shillings a month, twice that is twenty-eight; twenty-eight shillings a month, that is if Helen wanted two boxes a week. At this rate she'd be spending sixteen pounds sixteen shillings a year. Lord amassy! But perhaps Helen wouldn't want two boxes of chocolates every time they went out together— If she didn't, she'd want other things, and catching sight of a jeweller's shop, Albert called Helen's attention to a cyclist that had only just managed to escape a tram car by a sudden wriggle. But Albert was always unlucky. Helen had been wishing this long while for a bicycle, and if she did not ask Albert to buy her one it was because another jeweller's came into view. She stopped to gaze, and for a moment Albert's heart seemed to stand still, but Helen continued her chocolates, secure in her belief that the time had not yet come for substantial presents.

At Sackville Street bridge she would have liked to turn back, having little taste for the meaner parts of the city, but Albert wished to show her the north side, and she began to wonder what he could find to interest him in these streets, and why he should stand in admiration before all the small newspaper and tobacco shops, till she remembered suddenly that he had invested his savings in house property. Could these be his houses? All his own? and, moved by this consideration, she gave a more attentive ear to Albert's account of the daily takings of these shops, calculating that he was a richer man than anybody believed him to be, but a mean one. The idea of his thinking twice about a box of chocolates! I'll show him! and coming upon a big draper's shop in Sackville Street she asked him for a pair of six-button gloves. She needed a parasol and some shoes and stockings, and a silk kerchief would not be amiss, and at the end of the third month of their courtship it seemed to her that the time had come for her to speak of bangles, saying that for three pounds she could have a pretty one—one that would be a real pleasure to wear; it would always remind her of him. Albert coughed up with humility, and Helen felt that she had "got him," as she put it to herself, and afterwards to Joe Mackins. So he parted easily, Joe remarked, and pushing Helen aside he began to whip up the *ré-moulade*, that had begun to show signs of turning, saying he'd have the chef after him. But I say, old girl, since he's coughing up so easily you might bring me something back; and a briar-wood pipe and a pound or two of tobacco seemed the least she might obtain for him. And Helen answered that to get these she would have to ask Albert for money. And why shouldn't you? Joe returned. Ask him for a thin 'un, and mayhap he'll give you a thick 'un. It's the first quid that's hard to get; every time after it's like shelling peas. Do you think he's that far gone on me? Helen asked. Well, don't you?

Why should he give you these things if he wasn't? Joe answered. Joe asked her of what she was thinking, and she replied that it was hard to say: she had walked out with many a man before but never with one like Albert Nobbs. In what way is he different? Joe asked. Helen was perplexed in her telling of Albert Nobbs's slackness. You mean that he doesn't pull you about, Joe rapped out; and she answered that there was something of that in it. All the same, she continued, that isn't the whole of it. I've been out before with men that didn't pull me about, but he seems to have something on his mind, and half the time he's thinking. Well, what does it matter, Joe asked, so long as there is coin in the pocket and so long as you have a hand to pull it out? Helen didn't like this description of Albert Nobbs's courtship, and the words rose to her lips to tell Joseph that she didn't want to go out any more with Albert, that she was tired of her job, but the words were quelled on her lips by a remark from Joe. Next time you go out with him work him up a bit and see what he is made of; just see if there's a sting in him or if he is no better than a capon. A capon! and what is a capon? she asked. A capon is a cut fowl. He may be like one. You think that, do you? she answered, and resolved to get the truth of the matter next time they went out together. It did seem odd that Albert should be willing to buy presents and not want to kiss her. In fact, it was more than odd. It might be as Joe had said. I might as well go out with my mother. Now what did it all mean? Was it a blind? Some other girl that he— Not being able to concoct a sufficiently reasonable story, Helen relinquished the attempt, without, however, regaining control of her temper, which had begun to rise, and which continued to boil up in her and overflow until her swarthy face was almost ugly. I'm beginning to feel ugly towards him, she said to herself. He is either in love with me or he's— And trying to discover his purpose, she descended the staircase, saying to herself: Now Albert must know that I'm partial to Joe Mackins. It can't be that he doesn't suspect. Well, I'm damned.

4

But Helen's perplexity on leaving the hotel was no greater than Albert's as she stood waiting by the kerb. She knew that Helen carried on with Joe Mackins, and she also knew that Joe Mackins had nothing to offer Helen but himself. She even suspected that some of the money she had given to Helen had gone to purchase pipes and tobacco for Joe: a certain shrewdness is not inconsistent with innocence, and it didn't trouble her much that Helen was perhaps having her fling with Joe Mackins. She didn't want Helen to fall into evil ways, but it was better for her to have her fling before than after marriage. On the other hand, a woman that had been bedded might be dissatisfied to settle down with another woman, though the home offered her was better than she could get from a man. She might hanker for children, which was only natural, and Albert felt that she would like a child as well as another. A child might be arranged for if Helen wanted one, but it would never do to have the father hanging about the shop: he would have to be got rid of as soon as Helen was in the family way. But could he be got rid of? Not very easily if Joe Mackins was the father; she foresaw trouble and would prefer another father, almost any other. But why trouble herself about the father of Helen's child before she knew whether Helen would send Joe packing? which she'd have to do clearly if they were to wed—she and Helen. Their wedding was what she had to look to, whether she should confide her sex to Helen tonight or wait. Why not tonight as well as tomorrow night? she asked herself. But how would she tell it to Helen? Blurt it out—I've something to tell you, Helen. I'm not a man, but a woman like yourself. No, that wouldn't do. How did Hubert tell her wife she was a woman? If she had only asked she'd have been spared all this trouble. After hearing Hubert's story she should have said: I've something to ask you; but sleep was so heavy on their eyelids that they couldn't think any more and both of them were falling asleep, which wasn't to be wondered at, for they had been talking for hours. It was on her mind to ask how her wife found out. Did Hubert tell her or did the wife— Albert's modesty prevented her from pursuing the subject; and she turned on herself, saying that she could not leave Helen to find out she was a woman; of that she was certain, and of that only. She'd have to tell Helen that. But should the confession come before they were married, or should she reserve it for the wedding night in the bridal chamber on the edge of the bed afterwards? If it were not for Helen's violent temper— I in my nightshirt, she in her nightgown. On the other hand, she might quieten down after an outburst and begin to see that it might be very much to her advantage to accept the situation, especially if a hope were held out to her of a child by Joe Mackins in two years' time; she'd have to agree to wait till then, and in two years Joe would probably be after another girl. But if she were to cut up rough and do me an injury! Helen might call the neighbours in, or the policeman, who'd take them both to the station. She'd have to return to Liverpool or to Manchester. She didn't know what the penalty would be for marrying one of her own sex. And her thoughts wandered on to the morning boat.

One of the advantages of Dublin is that one can get out of it as easily as any other city. Steamers were always leaving, morning and evening; she didn't know how many, but a great many. On the other hand, if she took the straight course and confided her sex to Helen before the marriage, Helen might promise not to tell; but she might break her promise; life in Morrison's Hotel would be unendurable, and she'd have to endure it. What a hue and cry! But one way was as bad as the other. If she had only asked Hubert Page! but she hadn't a thought at the time of going to do likewise. What's one man's meat is another man's poison, and she began to regret Hubert's confession to her. If it hadn't been for that flea she wouldn't be in this mess; and she was deep in it! Three month's company isn't a day, and everybody in Morrison's Hotel asking whether she or Joe Mackins would be the winner, urging her to make haste else Joe would come with a rush at the finish. A lot of racing talk that she didn't understand—or only half. If she could get out of this mess somehow— But it was too late. She must go through with it. But how? A different sort of girl altogether was needed, but she liked Helen. Her way of standing on a doorstep, her legs a little apart, jawing a tradesman, and she'd stand up to Mrs. Baker and to the chef himself. She liked the way Helen's eyes lighted up when a thought came into her mind; her cheery laugh warmed Albert's heart as nothing else did. Before she met Helen she often feared her heart was growing cold. She might try the world over and not find one that would run the shop she had in mind as well as Helen. But the shop wouldn't wait; the owners of the shop would withdraw their offer if it was not accepted before next Monday. And today is Friday, Albert said to herself. This evening or never. Tomorrow Helen'll be on duty all day; on Sunday she'll contrive some excuse to get out to meet Joe Mackins. After all, why not this evening? for what must be had better be faced bravely; and while the tram rattled down the long street, Rathmines Avenue, past the small houses atop of high steps, pretty boxes with ornamental trees in the garden, some with lawns, with here and there a more substantial house set in the middle of three or four fields at least, Albert meditated, plan after plan rising up in her mind; and when the car turned to the right and then to the left and proceeded at a steady pace up the long incline, Rathgar Avenue, Albert's courage was again at ebb. All the subterfuges she had woven— the long discussion in which she would maintain that marriage should not be considered as a sexual adventure, but a community of interests—seemed to have lost all significance; the points that had seemed so convincing in Rathmines Avenue were forgotten in Rathgar Avenue, and at Terenure she came to the conclusion that there was no use trying to think the story out beforehand; she would have to adapt her ideas to the chances that would arise as they talked under the trees in the dusk in a comfortable hollow, where they could lie at length out of hearing of the other lads and lasses whom they would find along the banks, resting after the labour of the day in dim contentment, vaguely conscious of each other, satisfied with a vague remark, a kick or a push.

It was the hope that the river's bank would tempt him into confidence that had suggested to Helen that they might spend the evening by the Dodder. Albert had welcomed the suggestion, feeling sure that if there was a place in the world that would make the telling of her secret easy it was the banks of the Dodder; and she was certain she would be able to speak it in the hollow under the ilex trees. But speech died from her lips, and the silence round them seemed sinister and foreboding. She seemed to dread the river flowing over its muddy bottom, without ripple or eddy; and she started when Helen asked her of what she was thinking. Albert answered: Of you, dear; and how pleasant it is to be sitting with you. On these words the silence fell again, and Albert tried to speak, but her tongue was too thick in her mouth; she felt like choking, and the silence was not broken for some seconds, each seeming a minute. At last a lad's voice was heard: I'll see if you have any lace on your drawers; and the lass answered: You shan't. There's a pair that's enjoying themselves, Helen said, and she looked upon the remark as fortunate, and hoped it would give Albert the courage to pursue his courtship. Albert, too, looked upon the remark as fortunate, and she tried to ask if there was lace on all women's drawers; and meditated a reply that would lead her into a confession of her sex. But the words: It's so long since I've worn any, died on her lips; and instead of speaking these words she spoke of the Dodder, saying: What a pity it isn't nearer Morrison's. Where would you have it? Helen replied— flowing down Sackville Street into the Liffey? We should be lying there as thick as herrings, without room to move, or we should be unable to speak to each other without being overheard. I dare say you are right, Albert answered, and she was so frightened that she added: But we have to be back at eleven o'clock, and it takes an hour to get there. We can go back now if you like, Helen rapped out. Albert apologised, and hoping that something would happen to help her out of her difficulty, she began to represent Morrison's Hotel as being on the whole advantageous to servants. But Helen did not respond. She seems to be getting angrier and angrier, Albert said to herself, and she asked, almost in despair, if the Dodder was pretty all the way down to the sea. And remembering a walk with Joe, Helen answered: There are woods as far as Dartry—the Dartry Dye Works, don't you know them? But I don't think there are any very pretty spots. You know Ring's End, don't you? Albert said she had been there once; and Helen spoke of a large three-masted vessel that she had seen some Sundays ago by the quays. You were there with Joe Mackins, weren't you? Well, what if I was? Only this, Albert answered, that I don't think it is usual for a girl to keep company with two chaps, and I thought— Now, what did you think? Helen said. That you didn't care for me well enough— For what? she asked. You know we've been going out for three months, and it doesn't seem natural to keep talking always, never wanting to put your arm round a girl's waist. I suppose Joe isn't like me, then? Albert asked; and Helen laughed, a scornful little laugh. But, Albert went on, isn't the time for kissing when one is wedded? This is the first time you've said anything about marriage, Helen rapped out. But I thought there had always been an understanding between us, said Albert, and it's only now I can tell you what I have to offer. The words were well chosen. Tell me about it, Helen said, her eyes and voice revealing her cupidity to Albert, who continued all the same to unfold her plans, losing herself in details that bored Helen, whose thoughts returned to the dilemma she was in—to refuse Albert's offer or to break with Joe; and that she should be obliged to do either one or the other was a disappointment to her. All you say about the shop is right enough, but it isn't a very great compliment to a girl. What, to ask her to marry? Albert interjected. Well, no, not if you haven't kissed her first. Don't speak so loud, Albert whispered; I'm sure that couple heard what you said, for they went away laughing. I don't care whether they laughed or cried, Helen answered. You don't want to kiss me, do you? and I don't want to marry a man who isn't in love with me. But I do want to kiss you, and Albert bent down and kissed Helen on both cheeks. Now you can't say I haven't kissed you, can you? You don't call that kissing, do you?

Helen asked. But how do you wish me to kiss you, Helen? Well, you are an innocent! she said, and she kissed Albert vindictively. Helen, leave go of me; I'm not used to such kisses. Because you're not in love, Helen replied. In love? Albert repeated. I loved my old nurse very much, but I never-wished to kiss her like that. At this Helen exploded with laughter. So you put me in the same class with your old nurse! Well, after that! Come, she said, taking pity upon Albert for a moment, are you or are you not in love with me? I love you deeply, Helen, Albert said. Love? she repeated: the men who have walked out with me were in love with me— In love, Albert repeated after her. I'm sure I love you. I like men to be in love with me, she answered. But that's like an animal, Helen. Whatever put all that muck in your head? I'm going home, she replied, and rose to her feet and started out on the path leading across the darkening fields. You're not angry with me, Helen? Angry? No, I'm not angry with you; you're a fool of a man, that's all. But if you think me a fool of a man, why did you come out this evening to sit under those trees? And why have we been keeping

company for the last three months, Albert continued, going out together every week? You didn't
always think me a fool of a man, did you? Yes, I
did, she answered; and Albert asked Helen for a
reason for choosing her company. Oh, you bother
me asking reasons for everything, Helen said. But
why did you make me love you? Albert asked.
Well, if I did, what of it? and as for walking out
with you, you won't have to complain of that any
more. You don't mean, Helen, that we are never
going to walk out again? Yes, I do, she said sul-
lenly. You mean that for the future you'll be walking out with Joe Mackins, Albert lamented. That's
my business, she answered. By this time they were
by the stile at the end of the field, and in the next
field there was a hedge to get through and a
wood, and the little path they followed was full of
such vivid remembrances that Albert could not
believe that she was treading it with Helen for the
last time, and besought Helen to take back the
words that she would never walk out with her
again.

* * *

The tram was nearly empty and they sat at the far end, close together, Albert beseeching Helen not to cast her off. If I've been stupid today, Albert pleaded, it's because I'm tired of the work in the hotel; I shall be different when we get to Lisdoonvarna: we both want a change of air; there's nothing like the salt water and the cliffs of Clare to put new spirits into a man. You will be different and I'll be different; everything will be different. Don't say no, Helen; don't say no. I've looked forward to this week in Lisdoonvarna, and Albert urged the expense of the lodgings she had already engaged. We shall have to pay for the lodgings; and there's the new suit of clothes that has just come back from the tailor's; I've looked forward to wearing it, walking with you in the strand, the waves crashing up into cliffs, with green fields among them, I've been told! We shall see the ships passing and wonder whither they are going. I've bought three neckties and some new shirts, and what good will these be to me if you'll not come to Lisdoonvarna with me? The lodgings will have to be paid for, a great deal of money, for I said in my letter we shall want two bedrooms. But there need only be one bedroom; but perhaps I shouldn't have spoken like that. Oh, don't talk to me about Lisdoonvarna, Helen answered. I'm not going to Lisdoonvarna with you. But what is to become of the hat I have ordered for you? Albert asked; the hat with the big feather in it; and I've bought stockings and shoes for you. Tell me, what shall I do with these, and with the gloves? Oh, the waste of money and the heart-breaking! What shall I do with the hat? Albert repeated. Helen didn't answer at once. Presently she said: You can leave the hat with me. And the stockings? Albert asked. Yes, you can leave the stockings. And the shoes? Yes, you can leave the shoes too. Yet you won't go to Lisdoonvarna with me? No, she said, I'll not go to Lisdoonvarna with you. But you'll take the presents? It was to please you I said I would take them, because I thought it would be some satisfaction to you to know that they wouldn't be wasted. Not wasted? Albert repeated. You'll wear them when you go out with Joe Mackins. Oh, well, keep your presents. And then the dispute took a different turn, and was continued until they stepped out of the tram at the top of Dawson Street. Albert continued to plead all the way down Dawson Street, and when they were within twenty yards of the hotel, and she saw Helen passing away from her for ever into the arms of Joe Mackins, she begged Helen not to leave her. We cannot part like this, she cried; let us walk up and down the street from Nassau Street to Clare Street, so that we may talk things over and do nothing foolish. You see, Albert began, I had set my heart on driving on an outside car to the Broadstone with you, and catching a train, and the train going into lovely country, arriving at a place we had never seen, with cliffs, and the sunset behind the cliffs. You've told all that before, Helen said, and, she rapped out, I'm not going to Lisdoonvarna with you. And if that is all you had to say to me we might have gone into the hotel. But there's much more, Helen. I haven't told you about the shop yet. Yes, you have told me all there is to tell about the shop; you've been talking about that shop for the last three months. But, Helen, it was only yesterday that I got a letter saying that they had had another offer for the shop, and that they could give me only till Monday morning to close with them; if the lease isn't signed by then we've lost the shop. But do you think, Helen asked, that the shop will be a success? Many shops promise well in the beginning and fade away till they don't get a customer a day. Our shop won't be like that, I know it won't; and Albert began an appraisement of the shop's situation and the custom it commanded in the neighbourhood and the possibility of developing that custom. We shall be able to make a great success of that shop, and people will be coming to see us, and they will be having tea with us in the parlour, and they'll envy us, saying that never have two people had such luck as we have had. And our wedding will be— Will be what? Helen asked. Will be a great wonder. A great wonder indeed, she replied, but I'm not going to wed you, Albert Nobbs, and now I see it's beginning to rain. I can't remain out any longer. You're thinking of your hat; I'll buy another. We may as well say good-bye, she answered, and Albert saw her going towards the doorway. She'll see Joe Mackins before she goes to her bed, and lie dreaming of him; and I shall lie away in my bed, my thoughts flying to and fro the livelong night, zig-zagging up and down like bats. And then remembering that if she went into the hotel she might meet Helen and Joe Mackins, she rushed on with a hope in her mind that after a long walk round Dublin she might sleep.

* * *

At the corner of Clare Street she met two women strolling after a fare—ten shillings or a sovereign, which? she asked herself—and terrified by the shipwreck of all her hopes, she wished she were one of them. For they at least are women, whereas I am but a perhapser— In the midst of her grief a wish to speak to them took hold of her. But if I speak to them they'll expect me to— All the same her steps quickened, and as she passed the two street-walkers she looked round, and one woman, wishing to attract her attention, said: It was almost a love dream. Almost a love dream? Albert repeated. What are you two women talking about? and the woman next to Albert said: My friend here was telling me of a dream she had last night. A dream, and what was her dream about? Albert asked. Kitty was telling me that she was

better than a love dream; now do you think she is,
sir? I'll ask Kitty herself, Albert replied, and Kitty
answered him: A shade. Only a shade, Albert returned, and as they crossed the street a gallant at-
tached himself to Kitty's companion. Albert and
Kitty were left together, and Albert asked her companion to tell her name. My name is Kitty Mac-
Can, the girl replied. It's odd we've never met
before, Albert replied, hardly knowing what she
was saying. We're not often this way, was the answer. And where do you walk usually—of an evening? Albert asked. In Grafton Street or down by
College Green; sometimes we cross the river. To
walk in Sackville Street, Albert interjected; and she
tried to lead the woman into a story of her life. But
you're not one of them, she said, that think that
we should wash clothes in a nunnery for nothing?
I'm a waiter in Morrison's Hotel. As soon as the
name of Morrison's Hotel passed Albert's lips she
began to regret having spoken about herself. But
what did it matter now? and the woman didn't
seem to have taken heed of the name of the hotel.
Is the money good in your hotel? Kitty asked; I've
heard that you get as much as half-a-crown for

carrying up a cup of tea; and her story dribbled out in remarks, a simple story that Albert tried to listen to, but her attention wandered, and Kitty, who was not unintelligent, began to guess Albert to be in the middle of some great grief. It doesn't matter about me, Albert answered her, and Kitty being a kind girl said to herself: If I can get him to come home with me I'll help him out of his sorrow, if only for a little while. So she continued to try to interest him in herself till they came to Fitzwilliam Place; and it was not till then that Kitty remembered she had only three and sixpence left out of the last money she had received, and that her rent would be due on the morrow. She daren't return home without a gentleman; her landlady would be at her; and the best time of the night was going by talking to a man who seemed like one who would bid her a curt good-night at the door of his hotel. Where did he say his hotel was? she asked herself; and then, aloud, she said: You're a waiter, aren't you? I've forgotten which hotel you said. Albert didn't answer, and, troubled by her companion's silence, Kitty continued: I'm afraid I'm taking you out of your way. No, you aren't; all ways are the same to me. Well, they aren't to me, she replied. I must get some money tonight. I'll give you some money, Albert said. But won't you come home with me? the girl asked. Albert hesitated, tempted by her company. But if they were to go home together her sex would be discovered. But what did it matter if it were discovered? Albert asked herself, and the temptation came again to go home with this woman, to lie in her arms and tell the story that had been locked up so many years. They could both have a good cry together, and what matter would it be to the woman as long as she got the money she desired. She didn't want a man; it was money she was after, money that meant bread and board to her. She seems a kind, nice girl, Albert said, and she was about to risk the adventure when a man came by whom Kitty knew. Excuse me, he said, and Albert saw them walk away together. I'm sorry, said the woman, returning, but I've just met an old friend; another evening, perhaps. Albert would have liked to put her hand in her pocket and pay the woman with some silver for her company, but she was already halfway back to her friend, who stood waiting for her by the lamp-post. The street-walkers have friends, and when they meet them their troubles are over for the night; but my chances have gone by me; and, checking herself in the midst of the irrelevant question, whether it were better to be casual, as they were, or to have a husband that you could not get rid of, she plunged into her own grief, and walked sobbing through street after street, taking no heed of where she was going.

Why, lord, Mr. Nobbs, whatever has kept you out until this hour? the hall-porter muttered. I'm sorry, she answered, and while stumbling up the stairs she remembered that even a guest was not received very amiably by the hall-porter after two; and for a servant to come in at that time! Her thoughts broke off and she lay too tired to think any more of the hall-porter, of herself, of anything. If she got an hour's sleep it was the most she got that night, and when the time came for her to go to her work she rose indifferently. But her work saved her from thinking, and it was not until the middle of the afternoon, when the luncheon-tables had been cleared, that the desire to see and to speak to Helen could not be put aside; but Helen's face wore an ugly, forbidding look, and Albert returned to the second floor without speaking to her. It was not long after that 34 rang his bell, and Albert hoped to get an order that would send her to the kitchen. Are you going to pass me by without speaking again, Helen? We talked enough last night, Helen retorted; there's nothing more to say, and Joe, in such disorder of dress as behooves a scullion, giggled as he went past, carrying a huge pile of plates. I loved my old nurse, but I never thought of kissing her like that, he said, turning on his heel and so suddenly that some of the plates fell with a great clatter. The ill luck that had befallen him seemed well deserved, and Albert returned upstairs and sat in the passages waiting for the sitting-rooms to ring their bells; and the housemaids, as they came about the head of the stairs with their dusters, wondered how it was that they could not get any intelligible conversation out of the love-stricken waiter. Albert's lovelorn appearance checked their mirth, pity entered their hearts, and they kept back the words: I loved my old nurse, etc. After all, he loves the girl, one said to the other, and a moment after they were joined

by another housemaid, who after listening for a
while, went away, saying: There's no torment like
the love torment; and the three housemaids, Mary,
Alice, and Dorothy, offered Albert their sympathy,
trying to lead her into little talks with a view to
withdrawing her from the contemplation of her
own grief, for women are always moved by a love
story. Before long their temper turned against
Helen, and they often went by asking themselves
why she should have kept company with Albert all
these months if she didn't mean to wed him. No
wonder the poor man was disappointed. He is de-
stroyed with his grief, said one; look at him, without any more colour in his face than is in my
duster. Another said: He doesn't swallow a bit of
food. And the third said: I poured out a glass of
wine for him that was left over, but he put it away.
Isn't love awful? But what can he see in her? another asked, a stumpy, swarthy woman, a little
blackthorn bush and as full of prickles; and the
three women fell to thinking that Albert would
have done better to have chosen one of them. The
shop entered into the discussion soon after, and
everybody was of opinion that Helen would live to

regret her cruelty. The word cruelty did not satisfy; treachery was mentioned, and somebody said that Helen's face was full of treachery. Albert will never recover himself as long as she's here, another remarked. He'll just waste away unless Miss Right comes along. He put all his eggs into one basket, a man said; you see he'd never been known to walk out with a girl before. And what age do you think he is? I put him down at forty-five, and when love takes a man at that age it takes him badly. This is no calf love, the man said, looking into the women's faces, and you'll never be able to mend matters, any of you; and they all declared they didn't wish to, and dispersed in different directions, flicking their dusters and asking themselves if Albert would ever look at another woman.

It was felt generally that he would not have the courage to try again, which was indeed the case, for when it was suggested to Albert that a faint heart never wins a fair lady she answered that her spirit was broken. I shall boil my pot and carry my can, but the spring is broken in me; and it was these words that were remembered and pondered, whereas the joke—I loved my old nurse, etc.—

raised no laugh; and the sympathy that Albert felt to be gathering about her cheered her on her way. She was no longer friendless; almost any one of the women in the hotel would have married Albert out of pity for her. But there was no heart in Albert for another adventure; nor any thought in her for anything but her work. She rose every morning and went forth to her work, and was sorry when her work was done, for she had come to dread every interval, knowing that as soon as she sat down to rest the old torment would begin again. Once more she would begin to think that she had nothing more to look forward to; that her life would be but a round of work; a sort of treadmill. She would never see Lisdoonvarna, and the shop with two counters, one at which tobacco, cigarettes and matches were sold, and at the other counter all kinds of sweetstuffs. Like Lisdoonvarna, it had passed away, it had only existed in her mind—a thought, a dream. Yet it had possessed her completely; and the parlour behind the shop that she had furnished and refurnished, hanging a round mirror above the mantelpiece, papering the walls with a pretty colourful paper that she had seen in

Wicklow Street and had asked the man to put aside for her. She had hung curtains about the windows in her imagination, and had set two arm-chairs on either side of the hearth, one in green and one in red velvet, for herself and Helen. The parlour too had passed away like Lisdoonvarna, like the shop, a thought, a dream, no more. There had never been anything in her life but a few dreams, and henceforth there would not even be dreams. It was strange that some people came into the world lucky, and others, for no reason, unlucky; she had been unlucky from her birth; she was a bastard; her parents were grand people whose name she did not know, who paid her nurse a hundred a year to keep her, and who died with-out making any provision for her. She and her old nurse had to go and live in Temple Lane, and to go out charing every morning; Mr. Congreve had a French mistress, and if it hadn't been for Bessie Lawrence she might have thrown herself in the Thames; she was very near to it that night, and if she had drowned herself all this worry and tor-ment would have been over. She was more resolute in those days than she was now, and would have faced the river, but she shrank from this Dublin river, perhaps because it was not her own river. If one wishes to drown oneself it had better be in one's own country. But why is it a mistake? For a perhapser like herself, all countries were the same; go or stay, it didn't matter. Yes, it did; she stayed in Dublin in the hope that Hubert Page would return to the hotel. Only to Hubert could she confide the misfortune that had befallen her, and she'd like to tell somebody. The three might set up together. A happy family they might make. Two women in men's clothes and one in petticoats. If Hubert were willing. Hubert's wife might not be willing. But she might be dead and Hubert on the look-out for another helpmate. He had never been away so long before; he might return any day. And from the moment that she foresaw herself as Hubert's future wife her life began to expand itself more eagerly than ever in watching for tips, collecting half-crowns, crowns and half-sovereigns. She must at least replace the money that she had spent giving presents to Helen, and as the months went by and the years, she remembered, with increasing bitterness, that she had wasted nearly twenty pounds on

Helen, a cruel, heartless girl that had come into her life for three months and had left her for Joe Mackins. She took to counting her money in her room at night. The half-crowns were folded up in brown-paper packets, the half-sovereigns in blue, the rare sovereigns were in pink paper, and all these little packets were hidden away in different corners; some were put in the chimney, some under the carpet. She often thought that these hoards would be safer in the Post Office Bank, but she who has nothing else likes to have her money with her, and a sense of almost happiness awoke in her when she discovered herself to be again as rich as she was before she met Helen. Richer by twenty-five pounds twelve and sixpence, she said, and her eyes roved over the garret floor in search of a plank that might be lifted. One behind the bed was chosen, and henceforth Albert slept securely over her hoard, or lay awake thinking of Hubert, who might return, and to whom she might confide the story of her misadventure; but as Hubert did not return her wish to see him faded, and she began to think that it might be just as well if he stayed away, for, who knows? a wandering fellow like him might easily run out of his money and return to Morrison's Hotel to borrow from her, and she wasn't going to give her money to be spent for the benefit of another woman. The other woman was Hubert's wife. If Hubert came back he might threaten to publish her secret if she didn't give him money to keep it. An ugly thought, of which she was ashamed and which she tried to keep out of her mind. But as time went on a dread of Hubert took possession of her. After all, Hubert knew her secret, and somehow it didn't occur to her that in betraying her secret Hubert would be betraying his own. Albert didn't think as clearly as she used to; and one day she answered Mrs. Baker in a manner that Mrs. Baker did not like. Whilst speaking to Albert the thought crossed Mrs. Baker's mind that it was a long while since they had seen the painter. I cannot think, she said, what has become of Hubert Page; we've not had news of him for a long time; have you heard from him, Albert? Why should you think, ma'am, that I hear from him? I only asked, Mrs. Baker replied, and she heard Albert mumbling something about a wandering fellow, and the tone in which the words were spoken was disrespectful, and Mrs. Baker began to consider Albert; and though a better servant now than he had ever been in some respects, he had developed a fault which she didn't like, a way of hanging round the visitor as he was preparing to leave the hotel that almost amounted to persecution. Worse than that, a rumour had reached her that Albert's service was measured according to the tip he expected to receive. She didn't believe it, but if it were true she would not hesitate to have him out of the hotel in spite of the many years he had spent with them. Another thing: Albert was liked, but not by everybody. The little red-headed boy on the second floor told me, Mrs. Baker said (her thoughts returning to last Sunday, when she had taken the child out to Bray), that he was afraid of Albert, and he confided to me that Albert had tried to pick him up and kiss him. Why can't he leave the child alone? Can't he see the child doesn't like him?

But the Bakers were kind-hearted proprietors, and could not keep sentiment out of their business, and Albert remained at Morrison's Hotel till she died.

An easy death I hope it was, your honour, for if any poor creature deserved an easy one it was Albert herself. You think so, Alec, meaning that the disappointed man suffers less at parting with this world than the happy one? Maybe you're right. That is as it may be, your honour, he answered, and I told him that Albert awoke one morning hardly able to breathe, and returned to bed and lay there almost speechless till the maid-servant came to make the bed. She ran off again to fetch a cup of tea, and after sipping it Albert said that she felt better. But she never roused completely, and the maidservant who came up in the evening with a bowl of soup did not press her to try to eat it, for it was plain that Albert could not eat or drink, and it was almost plain that she was dying, but the maid-servant did not like to alarm the hotel and contented herself with saying: He'd better see the doctor tomorrow. She was up betimes in the morning, and on going to Albert's room she found the waiter asleep, breathing heavily. An hour later Albert was dead, and everybody was asking how a man who was in good health on Tuesday could be a corpse on Thursday morning, as if such a thing had never happened before. However often it had happened, it did not seem natural, and it was whispered that Albert might have made away with himself. Some spoke of apoplexy, but apoplexy in a long, thin man is not usual; and when the doctor came down his report that Albert was a woman put all thought of the cause of death out of everybody's mind. Never before or since was Morrison's Hotel agog as it was that morning, everybody asking the other why Albert had chosen to pass herself off as a man, and how she had succeeded in doing this year after year without any one of them suspecting her. She would be getting better wages as a man than as a woman, somebody said, but nobody cared to discuss the wages question; all knew that a man is better paid than a woman. But what Albert would have done with Helen if Helen hadn't gone off with Joe Mackins stirred everybody's imagination. What would have happened on the wedding night? Nothing, of course; but how would she have let on? The men giggled over their glasses, and the women pondered over their cups of tea; the men asked the women and the women asked the men, and the interest in the subject had not quite died down when Hubert Page returned to Morrison's Hotel, in the spring of the year, with her paint pots and brushes. How is Albert Nobbs? was one of her first enquiries, and it fired the train. Albert Nobbs! Don't you know? How should I know? Hubert Page replied. I've only just come back to Dublin. What is there to know? Don't you ever read the papers? Read the papers? Hubert repeated. Then you haven't heard that Albert Nobbs is dead? No, I haven't heard of it. I'm sorry for him, but after all, men die; there's nothing wonderful in that, is there? No; but if you had read the papers you'd have learnt that Albert Nobbs wasn't a man at all. Albert Nobbs was a woman. Albert Nobbs a woman! Hubert replied, putting as much surprise as she could into her voice. So you never heard? And the story began to fall out from different sides, everybody striving to communicate bits to her, until at last she said: If you all speak together, I shall never understand it. Albert Nobbs a woman! A woman as much as you're a man, was the answer, and the story of her courtship of Helen, and Helen's preference for Joe Mackins, and Albert's grief at Helen's treatment of her trickled into a long relation. The biggest deception in the whole world, a scullion cried from his saucepans. Whatever would she have done with Helen if they had married? But the question had been asked so often that it fell flat. So Helen went away with Joe Mackins? Hubert said. Yes; and they don't seem to get on over well together. Serve her right for her unkindness, cried a kitchen-maid. But after all, you wouldn't want her to marry a woman? a scullion answered. Of course not; of course not. The story was taken up by another voice, and the hundreds of pounds that Albert had left behind in many securities were multiplied; nearly a hundred in ready money rolled up in paper, half-crowns, half-sovereigns and sovereigns in his bedroom; his bedroom—her bedroom, I mean; but we are so used to thinking of her as a him that we find it difficult to say her; we're always catching each other up. But what I'm thinking of, said a waiter, is the waste of all that money. A great scoop it was for the Government, eight hundred pounds. The pair were to have bought a shop and lived together, Mr. Page, Annie Watts rapped out, and when the discussion was carried from the kitchen upstairs to the second floor: True for you, said Dorothy, now you mention it, I remember; it's you that should be knowing better than anybody else, Mr. Page, what Albert's sex was like. Didn't you sleep with her? I fell asleep the moment my head was on the pillow, Page answered, for if you remember rightly I was that tired Mrs. Baker hadn't the heart to turn me out of the hotel. I'd been working ten, twelve, fourteen hours a day, and when he took me up to his room I tore off my clothes and fell asleep, and went away in the morning before he was awake. Isn't it wonderful? A woman, Hubert continued, and a minx in the bargain, and an artful minx if ever there was one in the world, and there have been a good many. And now, ladies, I must be about my work. I wonder what Annie Watts was thinking of when she stood looking into my eyes; does she suspect me? Hubert asked herself as she sat on her derrick. And what a piece of bad luck that I shouldn't have found Albert alive when I returned to Dublin.

You see, Alec, this is how it was. Polly, that was Hubert's wife, died six months before Albert; and Hubert had been thinking ever since of going into partnership with Albert. In fact Hubert had been thinking about a shop, like Albert, saying to herself almost every day after the death of her wife: Albert and I might set up together. But it was not until she lay in bed that she fell to thinking the matter out, saying to herself: One of us would have had to give up our job to attend to it. The shop was Albert's idea more than mine, so perhaps she'd have given up waiting, which would not have suited me, for I'm tired of going up these ladders. My head isn't altogether as steady as it used to be; swinging about on a derrick isn't suited to women. So perhaps it's as well that things have fallen out as they have. Hubert turned herself over, but sleep was far from her, and she lay a long time thinking of everything and of nothing in particular, as we all do in our beds, with this thought often uppermost: I wonder what is going to be the end of my life. What new chance do the years hold for me?

And of what would Hubert be thinking, being a married woman? Of what else should she be thinking but of her husband, who might now be a different man from the one she left behind? Fifteen years, she said, makes a great difference in all of us, and perhaps it was the words, fifteen years, that put the children she had left behind her back into her thought. I wouldn't be saying that she hadn't been thinking of them, off and on, in the years gone by, but the thought of them was never such a piercing thought as it was that night. She'd have liked to have jumped out of her bed and run away to them; and perhaps she would have done if she only knew where they were. But she didn't, so she had to keep to her bed; and she lay for an hour or more thinking of them as little children, and wondering what they were like now. Lily was five when she left home. She's a young woman now. Agnes was only two. She is now seventeen, still a girl, Hubert said to herself; but Lily's looking round, thinking of young men, and the other won't be delaying much longer, for young women are much more wide-awake than they used to be in the old days. The rest of my life belongs to them. Their father could have looked after them till now; but now they are thinking of young men he won't be able to cope with them, and maybe he's wanting me too. Bill is forty, and at forty we begin to think of them as we knew them long ago. He must have often thought of me, perhaps oftener than I thought of him; and she was surprised to find that she had forgotten all Bill's ill-usage, and remembered only the good time she had had with him. The rest of my life belongs to him, she said, and to the girls. But how am I to get back to him? how, indeed? . . . Bill may be dead; the children too. But that isn't likely. I must get news of them somehow. The house is there; and lying in the darkness she recalled the pictures on the wall, the chairs that she had sat in, the coverlets on the beds, everything. Bill isn't a wanderer, she said; I'll find him in the same house if he isn't dead. And the children? Did they know anything about her? Had Bill spoken ill of her to them? She didn't think he would do that. But did they want to see her? Well, she could never find that out except by going to see. But how was she going to return home? Pack up her things and go dressed as a man to the house and, meeting Bill on the threshold, say: Don't you know me, Bill? and are you glad to see your mother back, children? No; that wouldn't do. She must return home as a woman, and none of them must know the life she had been living. But what story would she tell him?

It would be difficult to tell the story of fifteen years, for fifteen years is a long time, and sooner or later they'd find out she was lying, for they would keep asking her questions.

But sure, said Alec, 'tis an easy story to tell. Well, Alec, what story should she tell them? In these parts, Alec said, a woman who left her husband and returned to him after fifteen years would say she was taken away by the fairies whilst wandering in a wood. Do you think she'd be believed? Why shouldn't she, your honour? A woman that marries another woman, and lives happily with her, isn't a natural woman; there must be something of the fairy in her. But I could see it all happening as you told it, the maid-servants and the serving-men going their own roads, and the only fault I've to find with the story is that you left out some of the best parts. I'd have liked to know what the husband said when she went back to him, and they separated all the years. If he liked her better than he did before, or less. And there is a fine story in the way the mother would be vexed by the two daughters and the husband, and they at her all the time with questions, and she hard set to find answers for them. But mayhap the best bit of all is when Albert began to think that it wouldn't do to have Joe Mackins hanging around, making their home his own, eating and drinking of the best, and when there was a quarrel he'd have a fine threat over them, as good as the Murrigan herself when she makes off of a night to the fair, whirling herself over the people's heads, stirring them up agin each other, making cakes of their skulls. I'm bet, fairly bet, crowed down by the Ballinrobe cock. And now, your honour, you heard the Angelus ringing, and my dinner is on the hob, and I'll be telling you what I think of the story when I come back; but I'm thinking already 'tis the finest that ever came out of Ballinrobe, I am so.